A Note to Parents and Caregivers:

*Read-it!* Readers are for children who are just starting on the amazing road to reading. These beautiful books support both the acquisition of reading skills and the love of books. In some books, there are common sounds at the beginning, the ending, or even in the middle of many familiar words. It is good preparation for reading to help students listen for and repeat these sounds as part of having fun with words.

The RED LEVEL presents familiar topics using common words and repeating sentence patterns.

The BLUE LEVEL presents new ideas using a larger vocabulary and varied sentence structure.

The YELLOW LEVEL presents more challenging ideas, a broad vocabulary, and wide variety in sentence structure.

The GREEN LEVEL presents more complex ideas, an extended vocabulary range, and expanded language structures.

When sharing a book with your child, read in short stretches, pausing often to talk about the pictures. Have your child turn the pages and point to the pictures and familiar words. And be sure to reread favorite stories or parts of stories.

There is no right or wrong way to share books with children. Find time to read with your child, and pass on the legacy of literacy.

Adria F. Klein, Ph.D.
Professor Emeritus
California State University
San Bernardino, California

Managing Editors: Bob Temple, Catherine Neitge
Creative Director: Terri Foley
Editors: Jerry Ruff, Patricia Stockland
Editorial Adviser: Mary Lindeen
Designer: Amy Bailey Muehlenhardt
Storyboard development: Charlene DeLage
Page production: Picture Window Books
The illustrations in this book were prepared digitally.

Picture Window Books
5115 Excelsior Boulevard
Suite 232
Minneapolis, MN 55416
877-845-8392
www.picturewindowbooks.com

Printed in the United States of America.

**Library of Congress Cataloging-in-Publication Data**
Blackaby, Susan.
A pup shows up / by Susan Blackaby ; illustrated by Amy Bailey
Muehlenhardt.
p. cm. — (Read-it! readers classroom tales)
Summary: When Bob and the others go out for recess, a friendly dog joins
them on the playground.
ISBN 1-4048-0586-9 (hardcover)
[1. Dogs—Fiction. 2. Schools—Fiction.] I. Muehlenhardt, Amy Bailey, 1974-
ill. II. Title. III. Series.
PZ7.B5318Pu 2004
[E]—dc22                                            2004007388

# A Pup Shows Up

## By Susan Blackaby

## Illustrated by Amy Bailey Muehlenhardt

Special thanks to our advisers for their expertise:
Adria F. Klein, Ph.D.
Professor Emeritus, California State University
San Bernardino, California

Susan Kesselring, M.A.
Literacy Educator
Rosemount-Apple Valley-Eagan (Minnesota) School District

**PiCTURE WiNDOW BOOKS**
**Minneapolis, Minnesota**

The kids went outside for recess.

Kat played jacks.

Sunny jumped rope.

Jess shot baskets.

Vic pitched a ball to Bob.

Bob hit it into the trees.

A big dog ran onto the playground.

He had the ball in his mouth.

"Look, Mrs. Shay," said Bob. "We have a pup who wants to play with us."

"Be careful," said Mrs. Shay. "Dogs can bite."

The dog trotted over to Bob.

The dog dropped the ball.

He flapped his big pink tongue.

8

"He seems nice," said Bob.

Bob threw the ball for the dog.

The dog ran after it.

"I wonder where he lives," said Vic.
"Does he have a tag?" asked
Mrs. Shay.

Kat clapped.

The dog ran over to her.

She checked his collar.

"I do not see a tag," said Kat.

The kids played ball with the dog until he got tired.

Vic got the dog a dish of water.

Bob got scraps of food from

Miss Twist.

Jess put a rug in the ball box to make a bed.

Sunny led the dog over to the bed.

He flopped down for a nap.

"Can we keep him?" asked Kat.

"We can't keep a dog at school.
We will have to find his owner,"
said Mrs. Shay.

"He needs a name," said Jess.
"He has a lot of pep. Let's call
him Pepper."

"He squeaks like a mouse," said Vic. "Let's call him Pip."

"He has spots," said Bob. "Let's call him Spot."

"He seems glad to be here," said Kat. "Let's call him Happy."
"He found us," said Sunny. "Let's call him Lucky."

Just then the dog sat up. He barked at a lady wearing a big hat. She was walking across the school yard.

"Charlie!" said the lady. "There you are. I have been looking all over for you!"

The kids felt sad. The dog had a name. The dog had an owner. The dog had to go home.

"Thanks for taking good care of my dog," said the lady.

"We wanted to keep him for a while," said Jess.

"We thought he was a stray,"

said Bob.

Charlie wagged his tail.

"Most of the time Charlie stays with me," said the lady. "But on Fridays I have to go out."

"Sometimes Charlie gets lonely. He gets out of the yard. He looks for fun. Today he found you."

Jess rubbed Charlie's neck.
Kat scratched his ears.
"Maybe Charlie could visit
sometime," said Vic.

"I think that is a good idea," said Mrs. Shay. "On Fridays, Charlie can visit after lunch. We will not let him run away. We will play with him."

The lady thought for a minute.
Then she smiled. "I like this plan."

Charlie barked.

"Charlie likes it, too," said

Mrs. Shay.

# Levels for *Read-it!* Readers

**Read-it! Readers help children practice early reading
skills with brightly illustrated stories.**

**Red Level:** Familiar topics with frequently used words and
repeating patterns.

*I Am in Charge of Me* by Dana Meachen Rau
*Let's Share* by Dana Meachen Rau

**Blue Level:** New ideas with a larger vocabulary and a variety
of language structures.

*At the Beach* by Patricia M. Stockland
*The Playground Snake* by Brian Moses
*The Word of the Day* by Susan Blackaby

**Yellow Level:** Challenging ideas with an expanded vocabulary
and a wide variety of sentences.

*A Fire Drill with Mr. Dill* by Susan Blackaby
*Hatching Chicks* by Susan Blackaby
*Marvin, The Blue Pig* by Karen Wallace
*Moo!* by Penny Dolan
*Pippin's Big Jump* by Hilary Robinson
*A Pup Shows Up* by Susan Blackaby
*The Queen's Dragon* by Anne Cassidy
*Tired of Waiting* by Dana Meachen Rau

**Green Level:** More complex ideas with an extended vocabulary
range and expanded language structures.

*Classroom Cookout* by Susan Blackaby
*Clever Cat* by Karen Wallace
*Flora McQuack* by Penny Dolan
*Izzie's Idea* by Jillian Powell
*Naughty Nancy* by Anne Cassidy
*The Roly-Poly Rice Ball* by Penny Dolan
*Sausages!* by Anne Adeney
*Sunny Bumps the Drum* by Susan Blackaby
*The Truth About Hansel and Gretel* by Karina Law

**A complete list of *Read-it!* Readers is available on our Web site:
www.picturewindowbooks.com**